36

SUGAR CREEK GANG

The CASE OF THE MISSING CALF

Paul Hutchens

MOODY PRESS
CHICAGO

PREFACE

Hi—from a member of the Sugar Creek Gang!

It's just that I don't know which one I am. When I was good, I was Little Jim. When I did bad things—well, sometimes I was Bill Collins or even mischievous Poetry.

You see, I am the daughter of Paul Hutchens, and I spent many an hour listening to him read his manuscript as far as he had written it that particular day. I went along to the north woods of Minnesota, to Colorado, and to the various other places he would go to find something different for the Gang to do.

Now the years have passed—more than fifty, actually. My father is in heaven, but the Gang goes on. All thirty-six books are still in print and now are being updated for today's readers with input from my five children, who also span the decades from the '50s to the '70s.

The real Sugar Creek is in Indiana, and my father and his six brothers were the original Gang. But the idea of the books and their ministry were and are the Lord's. It is He who keeps the Gang going.

PAULINE HUTCHENS WILSON

1

This was the third worried day since Wandering Winnie, Little Jim Foote's white-faced Hereford calf, had disappeared. Though almost everybody in Sugar Creek territory had looked all over everywhere for her, nobody had seen hide nor hair of her. And as far as we knew, nobody had even heard her high-pitched, trembling bawl.

Different ideas as to what could have happened to the cutest little calf a boy ever owned had been talked about and worried over by all six members of the Sugar Creek Gang and by our six sets of parents. My own parents were doing maybe as much or more worrying than the Foote family.

As I said about a hundred words above this paragraph, today was the third worried day since Winnie had dropped out of sight. It was also the beginning of the third night. In a little while now, the Theodore Collins family, which is ours, would be in bed—just as soon as we couldn't stand it to stay up any longer.

Charlotte Ann, my little sister, had already been carried to her bed in the downstairs bedroom just off the living room, where Mom and Dad and I still were. Mom was working on a crossword puzzle, and I was lying on the floor piecing together a picture puzzle of a cowboy at a rodeo. The cowboy was trying to rope a scared-half-to-death calf. Dad was lounging in his favorite chair, reading the part of the newspaper Mom didn't have.

All of a sudden she interrupted my thoughts, saying, "Maybe we're all worrying too much about Winnie. Maybe she's already been found and is in some farmer's corral somewhere. If we wait long enough, somebody will phone for them to come and get her."

Dad, who must have been dozing, came to with a start and yawned a lazy answer. "Leave her alone, and she'll come home and bring her tail behind her"—which any boy knows is what somebody in a poem had said to somebody named Little Bo-Peep, who had lost her sheep: "Leave them alone, and they'll come home, bringing their tails behind them."

It was almost ridiculous—Dad's quoting a line of poetry like that at a time like that, because right that second I was on my hands and knees on the floor by the north window, looking under the library table for the part of the picture puzzle that had on it the rodeo calf's hindquarters. In fact, that last part of the calf was the very last piece of my puzzle. As soon as I could find it and slip it into place, the picture would be finished.

"What," Mom said to Dad from her rocker on the other side of the hanging lamp he was reading and dozing under, "is a word of seven letters meaning forever? Its first letter is *e,* and the last letter is *l.*"

Dad yawned another long, lazy yawn and mumbled, "What are the other five letters?" Then he folded his paper, unfolded his long, lazy legs, stood up, stretched, and said, "How in the world can you stay awake long enough to worry your way through a crossword puzzle?"

"I've got it! I've got it!" Mom exclaimed cheerfully and proudly. "The other five letters are *t-e-r-n-a.* The whole word is *eternal.*"

Dad, not looking where I was lying, stumbled over part of me but managed to keep from falling *ker-ploppety-wham* onto the floor by catching himself against the bedroom doorpost. He sighed a disgusted sigh down at me, saying, "What on earth are you doing down there on the floor! Why aren't you in bed?"

Looking at my picture puzzle, which Dad's slippered feet had scattered in every direction there was, I answered, "Nothing. Nothing at all. But I was looking for half a lost calf."

It seemed a good time for us to get ready to go to bed. When anybody is so tired that he is cranky-sleepy, he might lose his temper on somebody. And we had a rule in our family that everybody had to go to bed forgiven to everybody else.

Because, ever since I was little, I'd been giving Mom a good-night kiss just to show her I liked her, even when I was sometimes too tired to know for sure whether I did, I reached out my freckled left cheek for her to kiss. Looking at Dad, I gave him a shrug of both shoulders—which is a good enough good night for a father who has scattered his son's picture puzzle all over—and in a little while I was on my way upstairs to my room.

The window of that upstairs room, as you may remember, looks south out over the iron pitcher pump at the end of the board walk, over the garden to old Red Addie's apartment hog house, and beyond it to Little Jim's folks' farm. And over there was an empty corral with a whole calf missing, which calf might never come home again and bring her tail behind her.

I was too tired to say very much of a good-night prayer to God, but I knew that the One who made boys understood a boy's tired mind well enough not to expect him to stay on his knees beside his bed very long. Besides, anybody knows it's not how long anybody prays that counts with God, or what kind of words he uses, but whether he has honest-to-goodness love in his heart for his folks and for the Savior, who had first loved him enough to die for him. That was the most important thing my parents had taught me.

One of the very few things I prayed for before I clambered into bed was that Little Jim wouldn't have too hurt a heart because of his lost, strayed, or stolen white-faced, white-eyelashed calf.

And that—my last thoughts being about Wandering Winnie—is maybe why I had a crazy, mixed-up dream, the like of which I had never dreamed before in all my half-long life.

Honestly, that dream was so real it scared me half to death. It also seemed it wasn't a dream but was the actual truth. In fact, right in the middle of my dream, I dreamed that I woke up, and the rest of the dream seemed to be happening for sure.

I guess maybe the half calf I'd lost on the floor of our living room was part of the reason I dreamed what I did. Maybe the other reason was that on the way to the stairs, which was through the kitchen, I had stopped to eat the second half of a piece of peach pie that I had left over from supper and which Mom had promised me I could have for a bedtime snack.

Right in the middle of eating that very tasty piece of peach pie, I heard the radio going in the living room, and somebody's voice galloping along about all the things that were happening "in the world and here at home."

That was one of the last things Dad did every night—listen to the news, some of which was full of excitement and some of it not.

Just as I tucked the last bite of my piece of peach pie into my mouth and was starting upstairs to tuck myself into bed, I heard the news reporter say, "This program is being brought to you by the Kangaroo Sales Pavilion of Tippecanoe County. Remember—Saturday at one o'clock, thirty head of sheep, seventeen Hereford calves, fifty-three shoats, and . . ."

On the way to the top of the stairs, where

the moonlight was streaming in through the south window, I was still enjoying the taste of peach pie and was thinking what a good pie maker Mom was.

It took me only a few fumbling minutes to get undressed. When I finished my bedtime prayer, I yawned one of Dad's kind of long, lazy, noisy yawns, flopped over into bed, pulled Mom's nice fresh-air-smelling sheet over me, sighed a sleepy sigh, and started to sail off in a wooden shoe.

Did you ever have in your school reader the poem called "Wynken, Blynken, and Nod"? We'd had to learn it by heart when I was in the fourth grade. And it seemed that nearly every night, when I was getting into bed, a part of the poem would start yawning its way through my mind.

That very interesting poem tells about Wynken, Blynken, and Nod's getting into a big wooden shoe and sailing off on "a river of crystal light into a sea of dew." When the old moon saw them sailing along, he called out to them, asking where they were going and what they were looking for. And they answered, "We have come to fish for the herring fish that live in this beautiful sea."

Anyway, the writer of the poem—somebody I had never heard of, named Eugene Field—explained in the last verse of the poem that "Wynken and Blynken were two little eyes and Nod was a little head," and the wooden shoe was a trundle bed—whatever that was.

Anyway, after memorizing the poem, I'd always thought of going to sleep as sailing off in a wooden shoe.

In seconds, I'd climbed into my own wooden shoe and taken off. And that's when my crazy, mixed-up dream began spinning round and round in my mind.

First, I saw myself standing in our living room, looking into the long mirror on the wall above the library table, under which, as you already know, I had been looking for half a lost calf. All of a sudden then, while I was combing my red hair, I was seeing in the mirror not a red-haired, freckle-faced boy but a hornless, white-faced Hereford with long white eyelashes.

Quicker than a firefly's fleeting flash, in my dream I was over at Little Jim's place, and I was a red-haired heifer named Wandering Winnie, standing at the Footes' corral gate.

Racing toward me from behind was a cowboy on a pinto pony, swinging a lasso. And as calves do at a rodeo, I whirled and started to run like four-footed lightning to get away from him.

Then, in another fleeting flash, I wasn't a calf anymore but was Theodore Collins's only son. And the cowboy had turned into a masked rider, whose horse was big and black and had thundering hoofs.

"Help! Help! Help!" I yelled as I ran.

And then that masked rider's rope settled over my head and shoulders, the black horse skidded to a dusty four-footed stop by the iron

11

pitcher pump on our farm. And right then in the dream, the big black horse whirled and started to run, dragging me head-and-shoulders-and-face-and-neck-and-ears-first across a whole barnyard full of peach pies.

"*Help! Help! Help! Help!*" I kept on yelling. I couldn't get my breath. Also I couldn't turn over in bed, where suddenly it seemed I was, in my own upstairs room being choked half to death. I was screaming, but I couldn't scream very loud.

Well, right that crazy, mixed-up second, there was a voice coming out of somewhere up the stairway. It was my mother calling, "Bill Collins! What on earth are you yelling about up there? You having a nightmare or something?"

It seemed I was still out in our barnyard, being dragged headfirst through a thousand peach pies, while I was also still in bed, trying to turn over and wake up and couldn't.

Right away, though, I *did* wake up on account of my father's thundery voice joining in with Mom's worried one and ordering me to go back to sleep. Also he ordered me to turn over, as I was probably on my back—which I was and which most people are when they are having what is called a nightmare.

I made myself turn over, and pretty soon, without knowing I was going to do it, I set sail again for the land of Nod, and the next thing I knew, it was morning.

It was one of the most sunshiny mornings I ever woke up in. And the smell of bacon and eggs frying downstairs in our kitchen made me hungry—not for peach pie, though, which for some reason, it seemed, maybe I wouldn't want any more of for a long time. I wanted something salty instead.

Even while I was shoving myself into my shirt and jeans, I was looking out the south window to the grassy barnyard, where Dad, carrying our three-gallon milk pail, was coming toward the pitcher pump. Mixy, our black-and-white mother cat, was following along with him, meowing up at him and at the milk pail all the way.

At the pump, Dad stopped, lifted the pail out of Mixy's reach, and, shading his eyes, looked toward the sky. Then he called to Mom, who was maybe standing in the kitchen doorway right below my window, "Turkey buzzards are all over up there! Must be something dead somewhere!"

I stooped low, so that I could see under the overhanging leaves of the ivy that sprawled across the upper one-third of my window, and looked out and up toward where Dad had been looking. And what to my wondering eyes should appear but seven or eight wide-winged birds sailing like Wynken, Blynken, and Nod in a sea of dew—except that there probably wasn't any dew that high up in the sky on a sunshiny day.

I knew from the different buzzards I had

seen on the ground at different times, gob-
bling down dead rats or mice—or a possum or
coon or skunk some hunter had caught and
skinned—that buzzards were what Dad called
"carrion eaters."

Did you ever see a buzzard up close, maybe
only fifty feet away? If you ever get a chance to
see one on the ground, you will notice that he
is twenty or so inches long from his ugly head
at the top of his long, naked, wrinkled, scrawny
neck to the tip of his tail. And if while you are
watching him, he decides it's time to take off
on a trip to the sky again, you'd see that his
wingspread is maybe as much as six feet—as far
from the tip of one black-feathered wing to the
other as my tallish father is tall.

A turkey buzzard is the biggest, most awkward bird in the whole territory. He is also one
of the most important. Many a time I had
looked straight up into the straight-up sky and
seen one of those big black vultures soaring in
a silent circle, sometimes so high above the
fields or woods that he would look as if he was
maybe only ten inches from wingtip to wingtip.

Then, all of a sudden, he would come
shooting down in a long slant and land with an
awkward *ploppety-plop-plop, ker-flop-flop-flop* away
out in the field or maybe even close by.

In less than three minutes, another buzzard and then another and still another—as
many sometimes as five—would land *plop* at the
same place like black-winged arrows. And I
knew they had come slanting down out of the

sky to do what their Creator had made them for in the first place—to have breakfast or dinner or supper on a dead carcass of some kind. It could be a rat or a mouse or a possum or coon or skunk or even a horse or cow that had happened to die or get killed. So turkey buzzards were as important as any birds in the whole Sugar Creek territory.

"Don't you boys ever kill one of them," Dad had ordered the gang one day when he was also talking to us about being careful never to kill owls, because they were helpful to farmers by eating cutworms and mice. "A buzzard," he explained to us, "is one of nature's scavengers. Its business is to clean up the country and not allow any germ-breeding dead animals to smell up the clean, fresh country air and spread sickness or disease of any kind.

"Seagulls are scavengers, too," Dad went on.

But we didn't know anything about seagulls, there not being any in our territory, and nobody in the gang ever saw a seagull.

Well, because I was hungry, I quick finished shoving myself into my clothes and in a few minutes was downstairs.

At the breakfast table, Dad looked across at me, studying my face with a question mark in his eye, and asked, "What was your nightmare about last night?"

"It wasn't a nightmare," I answered, trying to be funny and maybe not being. "It was a night calf!"

It seemed all right to tell my folks what I

had dreamed, which I did. We also talked to each other about different things. It was a happy breakfast for the whole family except Charlotte Ann, my little sister, who wasn't in a good humor for a change.

And do you know what? My dream wasn't so crazy after all. Right that very minute, Dad reached up and turned on the radio, which was on the mantel beside our striking clock, just in time for us to hear the announcer say, "The Montgomery County sheriff's office reported late yesterday that two more calves were stolen in the area. The rustlers drove the calves out a gate near the Stonebergers' barn and down the lane to a parked truck where they were loaded on. This is the second case of livestock rustling in the county. Eighteen head of hogs were taken from the George Ranger's ranch last week . . ."

The news reporter went on then about something else, which gave my grayish brown haired Mom a chance to cut in and say, "Whatever is the world coming to—people stealing cattle and hogs right in front of your eyes on your back doorstep!"

Dad's answer wasn't exactly a surprise. It was what any boy who goes to church is supposed to know anyway, and it was: "The world isn't coming to anything, Mother. The world without God, which most of it still is, is already bad. The Bible says in Romans three twenty-three . . ."

And then the phone rang. Dad quick left the table to go answer it and started talking to somebody about a Farm Bureau meeting where he was going to make a speech about nitrogen and alfalfa roots—stuff like that.

When he came back, my deep-voiced, bushy-eyebrowed father was frowning a little about something somebody had said to him. Then he and Mom agreed with each other a while on what the Bible says about people's hearts and what is the matter with them.

My mind was on the news I'd just heard on the radio about rustlers having stolen two more calves right in front of our eyes on our own back doorstep. And it seemed maybe my mind was on the trail of an idea that would explain what had really happened to Little Jim's Wandering Winnie, so I didn't listen very well to what Mom and Dad were talking about.

But after breakfast, while I was out in the garden with the Ebenezer onions, the black-seeded Simpson lettuce, and the Scarlet Globe radishes, I was chewing over with my mind's teeth some of the words Dad had come back from the telephone with. Those words, word for word from the New Testament, were: "Out of the heart come . . . evil thoughts, murders . . . thefts, false witness . . ."

"The stealing of those calves was in somebody's heart first," I remembered he had said to Mom. "Then it was in the mind, and then he acted it out in his life. What can you expect from a sour crab apple tree but that it will bear sour crab apples?"

As I sliced away with my hoe, thinking

about something Dad had once told me—that I could keep the big weeds out of the garden by chopping them out while they were still little—I moved into the history section of my mind to the morning just three days ago when Little Jim had first missed his cute little white-faced baby beef.

But before I tell you what I thought and why, I'd maybe better let you know that, in the afternoon of the day I was living in right then, the Gang was going to have a very important meeting down at the spring near the leaning linden tree not far from the Black Widow Stump. I certainly didn't even dream what a lot of mystery we were going to stumble onto or that we'd find a clue that would shoot us, like six arrows out of a bow, into the exciting and dangerous adventure of finding out what had really happened to Wandering Winnie.

Boy oh boy, I can hardly wait till I get started into the first paragraph of that part of this story. What happened was *so* different from anything else that had ever happened to us in all six of our exciting lives.

Boy oh boy!

2

In case you are wondering how come Little Jim's white-faced baby beef was named Wandering Winnie, you might just as well wonder also how come she had quite a few other names.

Little Jim called her Wandering Winnie because she was always wandering away from their farm. Dragonfly, the dragonfly-like-eyed member of our gang, called her Winnie the Pooh, after a character in a children's book by that name. Poetry, the barrel-shaped, detective-minded member, who reads more books than any of us, had named her Little Dogie, explaining that "in the Old West, cowboys had a saying that a dogie was a calf whose mother was dead and his father had run off with another cow"—something like that.

You see, Little Dogie, Wandering Winnie, and Winnie the Pooh was an honest-to-goodness orphaned calf. Her mother had died about a week after Winnie had been born, and that made the calf a "dogie." Little Jim had bottle-fed Winnie until she was old enough to eat grass and bran shorts and other calf food.

Well, almost as soon as Winnie was a dogie old enough to run and gambol about Little Jim's barnyard, she had taken on a very bad habit. Having a wandering spirit in her heart, she was always running away from home.

Winnie never went very far, though. Most always it was over to our place. Sometimes as often as twice a week, when I would go out to our south pasture to drive Lady MacBeth, our Holstein milk cow, into her corral for Dad to milk her, I would find Little Jim's dogie lying in the shade of the elderberry bushes along the fencerow by Lady MacBeth.

Both of them would be lazily chewing their cuds, as if it was the pleasantest thing ever a cow and a calf could do. A black-and-white Holstein who didn't have a calf of her own and a white-faced Hereford who didn't have any mother would be lying side by side, doing nothing except maybe just liking each other. Mom, trying to defend Little Dogie, said that was very important even to a human being—just liking and being liked by somebody.

I guess maybe Mom felt that way about animals and people because in the Sugar Creek cemetery, not far from the church we all went to, there was a small tombstone that had on it the name of a baby sister I had never seen. She was born before I was and died when she was still little.

Mom had maybe one of the tenderest hearts for babies anybody ever saw.

Nearly every time I saw a contented cow lying on her side with her head up, chewing away, her eyes half closed as though she was almost asleep, I was reminded of a poem Poetry was always quoting. It had a line that ran: "Cows lie down upon their sides when they would go to sleep . . ."

Did you ever stop to think of all the different ways animals go to sleep? Our Mixy cat makes three or four turns round and round and settles down in a semicircle. Our old red rooster flies up to a tree branch or onto a roost in the chicken house and stands all night on one leg. A horse hangs its head and stands still all night in a stall.

And Lady MacBeth lies down on her side and spends all night chewing the food she has taken all day to eat too fast. Actually she swallows backwards every few minutes, doing it maybe a thousand times a night, and then the next day she starts in all over again. A cow is what is called a "ruminant," and all ruminants have two stomachs, one to eat into and the other to digest with.

One morning when I found Winnie lying on her side with Lady MacBeth, she had a cut over her left eye that was still bleeding a little and which she'd probably got when she came through the barbed-wire fence into our pasture.

Even as sorry as I felt for Winnie, I enjoyed running to our house, getting a special germ-killing salve we kept in the medicine cabinet, and dressing the wound, since I'm maybe going to be a doctor someday,

"You dumb little dogie!" I said to her in a playful scold. "Don't you ever let me catch you getting cut on that barbed wire again!"

Then I patted her on her hornless head and phoned Little Jim to come and get his cute little calf.

Just to be sure she wouldn't get cut again, I went down to our lane fence to the place where Winnie had been squeezing through and wrapped the barbed wire with a strip of burlap I tore from one of the gunnysacks we had in the barn.

Well, while I was in the history section of my mind out in our garden with the Ebenezer onions, the black-seeded Simpson lettuce, and the Scarlet Globe radishes, I was remembering that morning just three days ago when Little Dogie—Wandering Winnie the Pooh—had disappeared.

Little Jim had come pedaling over to our house on his bike, bringing with him a three-foot-long, yellow-barked willow switch, planning to do with the switch what I knew he'd done a half-dozen other times that summer—drive his white-faced, long-eyelashed, dumb dogie back home to her corral again.

That morning, three days ago, Lady Mac-Beth was already in *her* corral, already milked. She was waiting for me to turn her out to pasture again, where she would eat all day, so she could chew all night, so she could make white milk and yellow butter out of the brown bran and green grass she would eat.

The Collins family was at the breakfast table at the time, eating pancakes and sausage and stuff.

Hearing a noise out at our front gate, I looked across the table past Mom's grayish brown hair and through the screened side door of our kitchen. I saw Little Jim leaning his bike against the walnut tree just inside the gate. Then he went scooting across the lawn toward our barnyard and the pasture bars, carrying the willow switch. Even from as far away as I was, I could see the little guy had a very set face, as though his temper was up and he couldn't wait to explode it on Winnie.

In the middle of the barnyard, Little Jim stopped, looked toward the south pasture, and let out two or three long cow calls, which any farm boy knows sound like *"Swoo-ooo-ook! Sw-o-o-o-o-o-o-o-ook!"*

I was pretty soon out of my place without being excused, which is impolite to do, and was out the side door, letting it slam behind me—and shouldn't have or it might wake up Charlotte Ann. In a barefoot flash I was hurrying down the board walk and past the iron pitcher pump to where Little Jim was.

His set face was flushed from having pedaled so hard, his eyebrows were down, and he was as angry as I had ever seen him. He nearly always doesn't get angry at anything.

As soon as I reached the center of the barnyard, where Little Jim was, I said to him, "'S'matter? How come you're yelling like that at nothing?"

"I'm not yelling at nothing!" Little Jim Foote disagreed crossly. "It's Wandering Winnie the Pooh. That dumb dogie has run away again, and when I find her I'm going to give her a switching she'll never forget as long as she lives! You seen anything of her?"

I hadn't, of course, and neither had anybody else at our house. When I said so, Little Jim asked, "Where on earth can she be?"

What he said next got mixed up in my mind with something that was happening out by our garden gate right then—something I'd seen and heard happen maybe a hundred times that spring and summer. Old Red, our Rhode Island Red rooster, had just flown up to the top of the gatepost and was arching his long, proud neck, standing on tiptoe and getting ready to crow.

Hardly realizing what I was doing, I quickly stooped, grabbed up a roundish stone from the ground, and slung it toward the post. Even while that small round stone was flying through the air with the greatest of ease, Old Red was in the middle of his proud *"Cock-a-doodle-doo."*

Wham! The stone landed with a thud against the locust post just below Old Red's yellow legs, interrupting his ordinarily long, squawking *cock-a-doodle,* stopping it before it was half done, and scaring the early morning daylights out of him.

Old Red made a jump straight up, his wings flapping and his voice complaining, and came down *ker-floppety-plop* on the other side of the garden fence in the middle of the Ebenezers.

But Old Red wasn't any more scared right

then than I was. *What*—my stirred-up worry yelled at me inside me—*what if either of my parents comes to at the kitchen table and comes storming out to see what on earth is going on and why?*

Little Jim had already finished saying what he had started to say. I had heard his words without hearing them, but I did remember them later.

Quicker than a crash of thunder, I was off with an explosion of fast-running feet, galloping toward the garden gate with Little Jim's words flying along with me. Those worried words had been: "What I can't understand is how Winnie got out! We had the gate shut tight all night, and it was still shut this morning when I went out to feed her!"

Well, when you are in a garden, zigzagging after a scared rooster who is running wild all over the black-seeded Simpson lettuce, acting as crazy as a chicken with its head cut off, which you are going to have for dinner—the chicken, I mean, not the head—when your mind and muscles are as busy as mine were, you hardly notice anything strange in what Little Jim said, something that had a mystery in it.

All the noise I was making at the garden gate and, especially, the noise Old Red was making were like the noise Santa Claus's reindeer made in the "Night Before Christmas" when "out on the lawn there arose such a clatter, I sprang from my bed to see what was the matter."

"You," I thundered at Mom's favorite Rhode Island Red, "stay *out* of the garden!"

Little Jim's temper was still up as he hurried back to the walnut tree to his bicycle. He was maybe fifty yards up the road on the way to Dragonfly's house to see if Winnie was there, before what he'd said came to life in my mind. The words I all of a sudden remembered were "We had the gate shut tight all night, and it was still shut this morning when I went out to feed her."

I should have guessed *cattle rustlers* right then, but I didn't. Instead I had to let three days pass by and have a dream about a cowboy lassoing me and dragging me across the barnyard, before all the different ideas came to a crossroads in my head. And it seemed maybe there had been honest-to-goodness-for-sure cattle rustlers in the neighborhood and that Winnie the Pooh had been rustled right out of Little Jim's corral and taken off to a sales pavilion or somewhere, nobody knew where.

The morning of that fourth day finally passed at our house, and the Collins family was flying around getting ready to sit down to the noon meal, which was going to be fried chicken, bread and butter, rice pudding, and other stuff Mom had made.

"Don't forget early supper tonight," Mom said. "It's Saturday, you remember, and tomorrow is Sunday. So we go to town early, come home early, go to bed early, get up early, and get to Sunday school on time without rushing."

It seemed I had heard Mom say that maybe a thousand times in my half-long life, so, when all of us were at the table and Dad was getting ready to ask the blessing, I said—and shouldn't have—"Not too long a prayer, Dad. We have to have early supper so we can go to town early, and get home early, so we can go to bed early, and . . ."

Dad's answer was kinder than he maybe felt in his heart. He looked with lowered bushy eyebrows at me and said, "Do I ever pray all the way through to supper time?"

His prayer was long enough to be thankful in words for the food and to ask the Lord to "bless the hands that have prepared it"—meaning Mom's hardworking brown hands. He also prayed for our church's missionary who was working in an orphanage in Korea.

Just before saying, "Amen," at the end of his prayer, Dad thought of something else, which was, "And help us to do what we can about the hungry orphans over there."

To Mom he said, when he finished and before unfolding his napkin and laying it across his lap, "It's like the new Sunday school song says:

'Look all around you, find someone in need;
 Help somebody today.'"

As serious as my mind was at the time, it was still hard to keep from thinking a mischievous thought, which right that second popped into my mind. It was: "How come, Dad, you always pray for the hands that prepare the dinner but never for the hands that dry the dishes after dinner?"

Dad looked at my already busy hands and said, "When they're clean, they don't need anybody to pray for them."

And for some reason I left the table and went outdoors to the washbasin not far from the pitcher pump and scrubbed my hands with soap, as I was supposed to have not forgotten to do in the first place.

Bit by bit and bite by bite, I managed to get Mom's fried chicken dinner into the history section of my life. Pretty soon I would be ready to meet the Gang at the place we had agreed on—near the Black Widow Stump, halfway between that well-known stump and the linden tree that leans out over the hill sloping down to the spring.

With a *swish, swish, swish* and a *scrub, scrub, scrub,* I brushed my teeth for the second time that day, dried the dishes for maybe the thirty-seventh time that month, and pretty soon was on my way.

Out across the grassy yard I loped, past the plum tree, on to and past the walnut tree near the front gate, through the gate and past "Theodore Collins" on our mailbox, and across the road. My bare feet didn't even stop to enjoy the feel of the fluffy white road dust I usually liked to go *plop-plop-plop* in. With a flying leap I was over the rail fence, sailing over the way I'd seen a deer do it in an Audubon film one night that winter at the Sugar Creek Literary Society.

My shirt sleeves flapped in the wind, and my brown bare feet raced *lickety-sizzle* along the path made by barefoot boys' feet. I ran and ran and ran. A great big blob of happiness was in my heart, because that is almost the pleasantest thing ever a boy could do—to fly along, as I was flying along, toward an afternoon of adventure in a boy's world.

And it is almost the most wonderful feeling ever a boy can have to know you are not running away from something your mother wants you to do, because you have already helped keep her from getting too tired by helping her with the housework.

I guess one thing that made me feel so fine was that this time I had not waited for Mom to ask me to help but had actually volunteered to wash those very discouraged-looking dishes in the sink, which, unless you actually love your mother, is one of the most unpleasant things ever a boy has to do.

As I galloped along the winding path, the new Sunday school song was singing itself in my mind:

Look all around you, find someone in need;
Help somebody today;
Though it be little, a neighborly deed,
Help somebody today.

Many are burdened and weary in heart,
Help somebody today;
Someone the journey to heaven should start,
Help somebody today.

All the way to the Black Widow Stump, my heart was as light as a last year's maple leaf in a whirlwind.

I hadn't any sooner reached our meeting place, plopped myself down in the long, mashed-down bluegrass, and started chewing on the juicy end of a stalk of grass than Poetry came sauntering along the path that borders the bayou. Poetry was one of my almost best friends, the chubbiest one of the gang, the one with the best imagination, and also the most mischievous. His powerful binoculars were hanging by a strap around his neck.

I rolled over and up to a sitting position, squinted my sleepy eyes at him, then plopped back again onto the grass. In a minute he was lying there beside me.

While we waited for the rest of the gang, I was wondering if maybe I ought to tell him about my last night's dream and what I thought I knew about what had happened to Winnie the Pooh.

Suddenly Poetry let out an excited gasp and exclaimed, "There's a wild turkey!"

"Wild turkey!" I came to life. "I don't see any turkey. Do you see a turkey?"

"Look!" he said, handing me the binoculars. "Away up there above the Sugar Creek bridge, maybe a mile high."

I looked where he said to look, scanning the sky with his binoculars.

"Buzzard," I said. "That's nothing but a turkey buzzard. I saw half a dozen of them this morning over the south pasture."

As you already maybe know, that was the way a buzzard found his breakfast, dinner, or supper. He just sailed around in a silent circle, his eyes searching the earth far below until he spotted something that looked dead enough to eat. Then he'd come slanting down, land on or near it, and that would be it. So what was special about a turkey buzzard or two sailing around in the sky?

But I had seen something else when I was looking through Poetry's binoculars. "If you want to see something really important," I said to my round friend, "take a look at that big yellow woolpack of clouds hanging above the swamp. You know what that means, don't you—clouds piling up like that in the afternoon northwest?"

"Of course, I know what it means," Poetry answered. "If they come this way and change into umbrella clouds and spread all over the sky, it's going to rain pitchforks and tar babies."

For a few minutes, while the buzzards kept on sailing around so high that without the binoculars they looked like swallows, we bragged a little to each other about the cloud lore we had been studying in a schoolbook the winter before.

Any boy ought to know about cloud formations so that he can tell whether it is going to rain or not without listening to the radio or looking under a doorstep to see if a rock is wet because of the humidity in the air.

"Another thing," Poetry rolled over in the grass and said with his back turned, "when a cumulus cloud like that is opposite the sun, it is yellowish white, but when it is on the same side as the sun, with the sun behind it, it is dark and has bright edges."

"Is that where they got the song 'There's a Silver Lining'?"

"Sure," Poetry answered, and his squawking, half-and-half voice began croaking away:

"There's a silver lining,
Through the dark cloud shining."

There was nothing exciting to do until the rest of the gang came, which pretty soon they did. We had a business meeting about different things boys have business meetings about, and different ones of us took turns looking through Poetry's binoculars. We also skipped flat stones across Sugar Creek's foam-freckled face and listened to ten thousand or more honeybees buzzing among the sweet-smelling flowers of the leaning linden tree.

We came to with a start when Little Jim, who had the binoculars at the time, cried out, "Hey, you—everybody! Your turkey buzzard is coming down! He's heading straight for the sycamore tree and the mouth of the cave!"

My eyes took a quick leap toward the sky, and Little Jim was right. I saw that big buzzard slanting toward the earth like a long black arrow.

"There's another one!" Circus, our acrobat, exclaimed.

"There's three of them!" Dragonfly shouted, his pop-eyes large and round and excited.

"Five of them, you mean," Big Jim, our fuzzy-mustached leader cried out. "They're all coming down!"

We watched five black-winged rockets drop out of their silent circles down toward the earth in the direction of the sycamore tree, near which is the mouth of the cave and beyond which is the Sugar Creek swamp.

"Something's dead down there," Dragonfly decided and sniffed with his crooked nose. "Smell it?"

His face took on a mussed-up expression, and he let out two quick long-tailed sneezes.

I sniffed too but didn't smell anything except the perfume of the creamy yellow flowers of the leaning linden tree. But I knew Dragonfly had a very keen sense of smell and could sometimes smell things the rest of us couldn't, having what his doctor called "very sensitive olfactory nerves." All of a spine-chilling sudden, a cold fear blew into my mind, and I thought I knew what those sharp-eyed turkey buzzards had spotted from their spaceflight.

They had seen—and maybe smelled too—somebody's dead white-faced heifer!

Wandering Winnie the Pooh! my sad mind

told me, and without waiting for anybody else to say it first, I yelled to us, "Come on, everybody. Let's go see what's dead!"

3

I hadn't any sooner called out to us, "Come on, everybody! Let's go see what's dead!" than I took off on the run, leading the way on the little brown path that paralleled the creek all the way from the leaning linden tree to the Sugar Creek bridge. The rest of the gang ran with, behind, beside, and in front of me, all of us in an excited hurry to find out what was what and why.

As I ran and panted and worried, my mind's eye was seeing a red-bodied, white-faced Hereford calf lying somewhere out in the swamp, maybe caught and killed by a wild animal such as the one you've probably already read about in the book called *The Killer Cat*.

"Wandering Winnie!" Little Jim sobbed behind me.

In only a few minutes, we reached the rail fence at the north road, climbed through the rails, dashed across the road and up the embankment on the other side, and went flying on.

At the branch, we leaped across a narrow place and galloped onward. In only another few minutes we would get to where we were going, and then we would find out what those turkey buzzards had left their silent circles for.

Would we really find Little Jim's dumb dogie killed and half eaten by some wild animal? Had she maybe wandered out into the swamp, got herself tangled in a wild grapevine, and strangled to death, or what?

In a little while we would know.

My mind was running ahead of our twelve fast-flying feet as they flew us on toward the place where we had last seen the turkey buzzards, just before they disappeared among the trees of the swamp. One of the things I thought was: *When those big black birds were away up yonder in the Wynken, Blynken, and Nod world, what had their keen eyes spotted down in our territory that made them come shooting down from so far so fast?*

After what seemed too long a time, we came puffing to a stop at the sycamore tree close to the mouth of the cave where we had had so many wonderful summer and winter experiences. One of those worrisome experiences had been one dark. spooky night when I was all alone and had got myself stuck inside the tree's hollow and, half scared to death, had had to stay a long time, listening to the ghostlike sounds that haunted the swamp at night.

The path through the swamp was cool and damp, and there was a dank smell everywhere as we swung onto it and followed each other along, Indian style.

In another few minutes we reached the spot not far from the center, where there is a large muskrat pond and where on one of its shores there is a little knoll we called the

Giant's Head. The "giant" had a lot of long, green, mussed-up hair, which, of course, was long, green bluegrass.

It was the sunniest place in the whole swamp, and nearly always we would plop ourselves down there on top of the Giant's Head to tell each other stories and to watch the wildlife in the pond. There would be muskrats making long V-shaped water trails as they swam back and forth across. There would be mud hens upending themselves in headfirst dives, looking for breakfast or dinner or supper on the bottom. There would be dragonflies like baby-sized airplanes, skimming along just above the surface of the water, starting and stopping, and darting off in different directions, looking for their own breakfast, dinner, or supper in the air. There would be lazy turtles with nothing to do all day but sun themselves on long, lazy logs that jutted out from the shores. Things like that.

The sounds in the swamp were as interesting to a boy's imagination as the things he saw. Right that minute, while my eyes were searching all over everywhere for the turkey buzzards, the tree frogs were having the time of their lives, making noise like a thousand boys blowing balloons at a county fair.

"You know what tree frogs whooping it up in the daytime means, don't you?" Poetry asked me, and when I said, "What?" he answered, "It means there's a lot of moisture in the air. Frogs like things wet, and damp air makes them happy, because maybe it's going to rain."

"Look!" Dragonfly's excited voice exclaimed wheezily. He was short of breath from running and maybe also because it was the beginning of his hay fever season. "There they are!"

And there they were! All five of those naked-necked turkey buzzards were helping themselves to the carcass of something or other.

I was almost afraid to look for fear I'd see Wandering Winnie or what would be left of her if it was Winnie.

Circus, as quick as if he'd been started by the starter's gun in a hundred-yard dash, sprang into a run toward where the buzzards were gorging themselves, shouting, "Shoo! Scat! Get away from there!"

The buzzards were not scared enough to take to the air, though, but hopped awkwardly away to a place about fifteen feet from the brown whatever-it-was.

The rest of us had also been running and yelling and screaming the same excited orders. All of us except Little Jim, that is. He held back, his eyes glued to something I myself had already seen—something brown, out in the center of where the five birds had just been.

"It's a gunnysack with something in it!" Big Jim announced from where he and the rest of us had just stopped.

We were on our side of the woven-wire fence that separated the safe part of the swamp from the dangerous side. It was a new fence our Sugar Creek fathers had set there to keep animals or human beings from accidentally straying off the path and out into the quicksand. Anything or anybody getting into it could sink all the way down to his hips and waist and shoulders and over his head to what would be the end of his life in this world.

Maybe you've read the book called *The Mystery Cave*. It tells how one night, before there was any protecting fence, the Gang had seen a man's head lying out there in the quagmire—except that the head had a man's body fastened to it, and the body itself was down under the quicksand. The man who was yelling for help at the time was old John Till, the neighborhood's alcoholic, who was also Big Bob Till's father. If we hadn't saved his life that night, he would have died before he became a Christian, which is the worst time in the world to die, our minister says, on account of then it's too late to repent and believe and be saved from your sins.

Big Jim was right. That brown something-or-other was a large gunnysack. It also had a hole in one side of it, and my startled and worried eyes saw something red the buzzards had pulled partway out!

I didn't get a chance to wonder much about what or who was in the gunnysack, because Little Jim let out a sobbing yell, crying, "It's Winnie! Look, everybody!"

Everybody was already looking and staring and wondering what on earth and feeling sorry for Little Jim, because what we were seeing was not only the red hide of a Hereford calf but a white face as well.

In my mind it was clear as a sunshiny day that somebody—maybe even a half-dozen somebodies—had stolen Little Jim's dogie, taken her somewhere and butchered her, stuffed her head and hide in a big gunnysack, carried or dragged the gunnysack here, and tossed her over the fence out into the quicksand.

Poetry's detective-like mind came up with the answer I myself was thinking right then, and his squawky voice said to us, "They thought she would land in the quicksand and sink down out of sight forever, and nobody would ever know what had happened."

"But they missed it," Circus cut in to say, "and the gunnysack landed at the edge of the mire instead of in it."

Dragonfly broke in then with an excited stammer. "And—and the turkey buzzards looked down and saw it and—and—and—and—" He stopped stuttering to sneeze three times in a fast row.

And that's when Little Jim said, "Whoever threw her out there had to be somebody who knows where the quicksand is! Somebody who knows the territory like a spelling book!"

That, my mind told me, was the truth. It *had* to be somebody who had a map in his mind, knew where Little Jim's folks lived, knew about the path that goes through the swamp . . .

I didn't dare say what my mind was also saying to me inside of me, and that was: *The rest of*

Wandering Winnie—the part that wasn't in the burlap bag out there—has maybe already been cut up into steaks and roasts and ground into hamburger and might even be in somebody's freezer somewhere.

I didn't dare say it, because of what it might do to Little Jim's heart. One of the meanest things ever a boy can do is to do or say anything that will give anybody a hurt heart.

While we were standing there looking through the woven-wire fence, and while the buzzards on the other side of the quicksand were waiting for us to get gone so they could come back and begin again on their lunch, Big Jim said grimly, "You're right, Little Jim. Whoever stole her and threw the gunnysack out there had to be somebody who knew the quagmire was here."

I was startled to hear Little Jim's quick answer, which he just then blurted out: "Bob and Tom Till didn't do it!"

"Nobody said they did!" Big Jim answered him, but I noticed his jaw muscles were working and his eyes were squinting as he focused them on the dead head of what had been the most beautiful white-faced heifer a boy ever saw.

We all knew that even though many people in our part of the county knew about the quicksand, nobody would know it better than the Till family on account of Old Hook-Nose's having almost lost his life there—though the gang didn't call him "Old Hook-Nose" anymore. Mr. Till was a brand-new person ever since he had become a Christian.

But Bob Till had been one of our worst boy enemies, and Little Tom, his red-haired brother, had been mine for quite a while, having whammed me in the nose and given me a black eye in the Battle of Bumblebee Hill.

But you just can't stand and think and wonder and worry for a very long time at one time —not if you are a boy. Your mind and muscles have to do something about something even if you don't have any idea what.

We began moving around in silent circles, studying the ground, looking for clues.

"Footprints!" Dragonfly, from about twenty feet away, cried. "Whoever was here was wearing boots! I'll bet he was a boy about my size! My foot just fits into the prints!"

Circus looked up from his own silent circle and scolded, "Hey, you! Don't do that! Don't step in those footprints! Wait'll we see what *kind* of shoes or boots or what!"

But already it was too late. Dragonfly had stepped into every one of the four tracks he had found in the mud beside the fence. Every single one of them! There wasn't a heel or toe print that was clear enough for us to tell what kind of boots or shoes whoever had been here had had on.

Look as we would and as we did, all over everywhere all around, we couldn't find another track that was clean enough to study. For a few disappointing minutes we kept on searching the ground like six turkey buzzards looking for something we could swoop down upon as a clue.

Then Big Jim came up with an idea. "At least we could study the gunnysack to find out whether it was a new one or an old one and what kind it was," he said. "And later maybe find out who bought it."

It was a good idea.

"How, though," Circus asked, "are we going to get it without risking our lives?"

It was a good question to which nobody had a good answer—not until we'd used our six minds on it awhile. And you could hardly believe what we came up with.

It was Little Jim who thought of it first. He had been looking through his tears at what the buzzards were waiting to come back and start scavenging on again, when it seemed as if somebody had turned on a light in his mind.

"Look!" he came out with. "See that long tree branch hanging out over the quicksand? Whyn't one of us just climb the tree, crawl out on the limb till he gets straight up over the gunnysack, and—if he had a rope with a hook on it—he could reach down and hook it onto the sack. Then he could bring the other end of the rope back, and we could pull the sack back to the fence."

"Anybody got a rope with a hook on it?" Big Jim asked us.

Of course, not a one of us had.

Poetry said, "Our house is the closest to here. Let's go home and get a rope. We can make a hook out of number nine wire and see what we can do."

That made good sense. It was the best idea anybody had thought of until then.

I guess maybe I should have guessed that that very hot, stuffy afternoon, *and* the big thunderheads we'd seen building up in the northwest away beyond the bridge, *and* the tree frogs' noisy choir practice meant that an old-fashioned thunderstorm was getting ready to happen.

Anyway, almost as quick as it would take a boy to say, "Jack Robinson Crusoe," there was a rustling of the leaves of the maples and elms and ash and willows and a rumble of thunder that was so loud and so close that it half scared me out of what few wits I had at the time.

"It's going to rain!" different ones of us said to the rest of us.

And it was. Really was.

Really did, I mean.

"Quick!" Big Jim ordered us. "Everybody beat it to the cave, or we'll be as wet as six drowned rats!"

Right that second there was a blinding flash and a crash of thunder. The rain came pouring down. It was as though the sky was an upside-down sieve with a million holes in the bottom.

Like greased lightning, six boys made a wild dash for the sycamore tree and the cave, where, if we could get there in time, we would be safe from becoming six drowned rats.

And, boy oh boy, it was a good thing we did run to the cave for shelter. If we hadn't, we might have missed finding the *clue*—one that set six minds to work on the mystery of the stolen calf at Sugar Creek.

If you'll keep on reading, you'll see what happened next—something I didn't even know myself, as twelve fast-flying feet carried us pell-mell toward a shelter in the time of storm.

And if you don't happen to know what *pell-mell* means, all you have to do is look it up in the dictionary. You will find out it means that, if you are running the way we were running right that minute, you are racing "in a headlong hurry."

I didn't know the word myself until Poetry, who reads a lot, asked me, "How do you like running pell-mell like this?"

I could tell from his tone of voice that he had just learned the word himself and wanted me to know he knew it, so I said, "What's pell-mell?" And he told me.

Anyway, while we were pell-melling ourselves through the thunder and lightning and wind toward the shelter of the cave—even while I was worrying about Little Jim's dumb dogie, wondering who would be mean enough to steal her and butcher her and do with the carcass what had been done to it—I was also very happy.

Any boy is happy when he is in the middle of something like what we were in the middle of right that exciting, stormy, helter-skelter, pell-mell minute.

4

Anybody only as far away as the sycamore tree, looking toward six boys sitting side by side just inside the mouth of the cave, could have imagined that cave's mouth was the wide-open mouth of some giant who had six lower teeth and no upper teeth at all.

What a storm it was! We could hear its roar and, through the rain that was coming down in blinding sheets, could see the little brown path that leads into the swamp. Now it *wasn't* a footpath but was a yellowish stream of excited water tumbling pell-mell into the shadowy trees and bushes and hanging grapevines.

"I'll bet those buzzards wish they had a nice cave like this to get into. What do you suppose they're doing out there now?" somebody asked.

Because none of us knew what a turkey buzzard does in a storm, we changed the subject.

I didn't know that Dragonfly, who was the next-to-the-shortest lower tooth, had pulled himself out of the giant's jaw, until I heard him call from back inside the cave, "Look what I found! Somebody's been *smoking* in here!"

We all came to with a start.

When I looked behind me, I saw that the little guy had taken the flashlight we always kept in a secret place in the cave and was shining it on something.

"Whoever the cattle thief was, he smoked cigarettes," Dragonfly said.

In a few seconds, we were all in a noisy circle, looking at what Dragonfly had found.

Big Jim held it between the forefinger and thumb of his left hand. I could tell from the way his eyes were squinting and his jaw muscles were working that he already had something serious stirring in his mind. A second later he said grimly, "Let's all think a minute and see what we come up with."

That was the way we nearly always did when we were studying a mystery and wanted to wring out of it all the best ideas there were— the way somebody wrings a dishcloth to get out of it all the sudsy water there is.

For maybe sixteen seconds we stood in a silent circle, while the storm roared on outside and while we all focused our eyes on that half-smoked cigarette.

Little Jim's idea was: "It's got a green filter," which it did have, and that made it different from every other kind.

"Green, yes," Poetry said, "but it is also red. There's lipstick on it!"

There wasn't much red on it, but there was some. Quick as a flash, I thought to say, "That means whoever smoked it wore lipstick, and that means she was a—"

"*Woman!*" the rest of the gang interrupted me to say.

We had three clues now: the footprints Dragonfly had covered up were small—just the size of his feet; the thief, if that's who had been here, smoked green-filter cigarettes and wore lipstick; and the lipstick made her a woman.

Poetry came up with another idea. "She was a mannish type of woman, on account of she would have to have powerful muscles to carry a gunnysack with a calf's hide and head in it."

Out of the corner of my eye I noticed Little Jim's innocent face wince as if Poetry's words had jabbed him in his heart.

Now we were like six excited hounds on the trail of a coon, a trail as fresh as if the coon had crossed in front of our noses only a few minutes ago.

A powerful-muscled woman who wore boots, who smoked green-tipped cigarettes and wore lipstick—that was the kind of person we were on the trail of.

Carefully, Big Jim took the cigarette stub from Poetry, who had it at the time, and wrapped it in a clean handkerchief he borrowed from Little Jim. "First, we find out what kind of lipstick it is," Big Jim announced. "Then we can start trying to find out where it was sold and who bought it. And also who in the territory—what woman, anyway—smokes green-tipped filter cigarettes."

Well, a Sugar Creek storm hardly ever lasts very long, so after maybe seventeen minutes, it began to calm down like a boy's temper when he is getting over being mad. The sun came out, and long shafts of light began to shine across the muddy path that led into the swamp. The wind stopped blowing, the leaves of the trees stopped their noisy rustling, and birds that were glad to be alive started singing. Robins especially, who are always happy after a rain, began whooping it up: *"Go jump in the lake, go jump in the lake . . . cheerfully, cheerfully . . . go jump in the lake."*

I hadn't planned to be the last one out of the cave, but for some reason I was. Maybe it was because Big Jim asked me to put the flashlight back in its secret hiding place behind the rocky ledge we all knew about. And maybe also that's why I was so startled when I spotted on the sand floor of the cave a folded piece of white paper. I gasped out loud.

I stooped, picked it up, and shoved it into my shirt pocket before anybody could notice. A secret plan was taking shape in my mind. I would show it to Poetry just as soon as I had a chance and get his detective-like mind to working on whatever it was.

Right now we had *four* clues. The thief was a powerful-muscled woman who wore boots, who smoked green-tipped filter cigarettes and wore lipstick, and she had accidently dropped a folded piece of paper on the floor of the cave.

Those clues were enough to make any ordinary detective decide he was on a really hot trail. And Poetry was as good as a detective any day. He and I had worked alone on more mysteries than any of the rest of the gang. Of course, we had got ourselves into more scary situations because we worked alone, but as anybody knows, there isn't a boy in the world that doesn't enjoy being in the middle of a whirlwindlike adventure, if it isn't too dangerous.

Say, did you ever see a small, funnel-shaped whirlwind moving through our south pasture, carrying a lot of last year's leaves, straw, chicken feathers, dust, dead grass, and stuff? If you have, you will know that one of the happiest things a boy can do is to run pell-mell from the pitcher pump out across our barnyard, zip through the pasture bars, with flying feet race into the middle of that whirlwind, and go zigzagging along with it in whatever direction it goes. You feel the wind in your face and your shirt sleeves flapping, and also, part of the time, you're fighting to keep the dust out of your eyes.

Anyway, the Sugar Creek Gang had been caught up in a whirlwind full of mystery and maybe even of danger.

If we tried to go back to the gunnysack now, we'd have to wade in almost ankle-deep mud in the little brown path. Also, because we couldn't do what we wanted to do without a rope with a hook on it and also because it was time to get home to help our folks with the Saturday evening chores, we left the cave and the sycamore tree and the swamp behind. Not the *mystery*, though. It was still in our minds, and we had to take our minds along with us.

"What'll we do about telling our folks what we know?" we said to each other when we came to the leaning linden tree, where we were going to part until our next meeting.

Big Jim suggested, "If we tell anybody, the news'll spread like wildfire, and the sheriff or the marshal and maybe even the whole neighborhood will go down to the swamp. Our mystery will blow up in our faces, and we won't have a chance to solve it ourselves. Come on, everybody! Let's make a vow."

So we did, making a sort of upside-down nest out of our twelve hands and promising each other not to tell anybody what we knew until we could agree on what to tell and when.

"Tomorrow," our voices all repeated in chorus after Big Jim, "we will meet here and go down to the swamp and do what we planned."

"Bill, you got a rope long enough at your house?" Big Jim asked.

"My mother's got a new clothesline still not put up," Dragonfly volunteered. "I'll bring that."

"My father's got a short chain with an iron hook on it," Circus offered.

Little Jim chimed in with a question then, asking, "Which one of us climbs up the tree and crawls out on the long, overhanging branch?"

For several seconds nobody said anything. The only sounds were the humming and buzzing of ten thousand honeybees that had come back to work again on the sweet-smelling creamy flowers of the linden tree, the robins ordering us to cheerily jump in the lake, and the noise of other birds having the time of their lives being glad the storm was over.

Big Jim's answer to Little Jim's question was a surprise, but it seemed the best answer. "We'll wait till tomorrow," he said. "Then we'll draw straws, and whoever gets the shortest one gets to go."

And that was that—a very worrisome that, at that.

All the way to our house, I was thinking about it. Also I had my mind on a folded piece of paper in my shirt pocket. I would show it to the gang tomorrow—after showing it to Poetry tonight when we all met again on Main Street in town.

I had better tell you, just in case you don't already know it, that the Gang and their folks nearly always went to town on Saturday nights to buy groceries and to walk around and talk. That's the way people do who live near a town the size of Sugar Creek—the mothers not being able to say to each other all they want on the telephone because ours was a party line. And any secrets on a party line are not secret very long, my grayish brown haired mother has said many a time.

At our front gate, Poetry swung onto his bike and was ready to start puffing his way down the road to their house, when I said to him, "Tonight at the fountain in town."

"Tonight at the fountain," he said, and with his tongue between his teeth he started pedaling himself down the road, while I closed the gate and went on toward the pitcher pump and the house, my folded piece of paper feeling like a lump of lead against my heart.

I knew that pretty soon I'd find out for sure what was written—or maybe printed—on it. There might even be a map of the territory. If there *was* a map, would it show Little Jim's house and barn, the corral where Wandering Winnie was kept, and the lane leading to our own place, where Wandering Winnie came to lie down on her side with Lady MacBeth and chew her cud with her?

In only a little while, I was in the house and a little later was on my way to gather the eggs. There wasn't a hen's nest anywhere on the place I didn't know about.

First, though, I had something important to do up in the haymow. As I set my right foot on the bottom rung of the ladder, I spotted old Mixy, our black-and-white cat, crouching under the north window. Her eyes were fixed on a corner of Dad's tool cupboard, and I knew she was doing what a good cat should—waiting to catch a mouse she had maybe heard under the cupboard. Then I went on up the ladder, my heart pounding a little because of what I expected to find on the piece of folded paper in my shirt pocket.

Straight to my secret corner I climbed, far up over the hay and down a little hay hill. I was going to keep a very special promise I had made to God once, which was that as long as I lived I would read something out of the Bible and pray every day.

I took my small leather New Testament out of its hiding place in a crack in one of the logs and, opening it, read a story about a boy who had gone fishing. Then the Savior and a lot of hungry people came along. Jesus borrowed the boy's lunch and with His power used the lunch of only five small biscuits and two sardine-sized fish to feed all the people.

As I read the story I happened to think that, if the boy had kept his lunch for himself, it could never have been used to feed so many others—and that a boy my age ought to be unselfish enough to give his heart and anything else he had to God, so other people could be helped. And one way to do it would be to do as a certain gospel song said:

Look all around you, find someone in need.
Help somebody today.

I took a minute to kneel down and pray about different things I had on my mind. Then I was off my knees, and in the light that came through a crack in the weatherboards I unfolded the paper I'd found on the sandy floor of the cave.

What a disappointment! For what to my wondering eyes should appear, not what I had expected but a list of things written in Little Jim's smooth, round, schoolboy-style handwriting. It was like a balloon being pricked with a pin.

I think I will write down the list for you, though, just the way Little Jim had written it himself, one word right under the other. Here, if you are interested in something that at the time certainly didn't seem important, is what I read:

1. Up at 7:00—breakfast
2. Surprise Mother by making bed
3. Practice piano 30 min.
4. Secret
5. Garden work and feed chickens
6. Make new arrow
7. 10:00—secret
8. 11:00—piano again—30 min.
9. 11:30—secret
10. 12:00—lunch. Surprise Mother by helping with the dishes
11. 2:00—Black Widow Stump and the Gang

And that was all—just a list of things a boy had to do. Each item on the list had been checked with a pencil except the one that said "2:00—Black Widow Stump and the Gang," which meant that the little guy had planned his day in advance and one by one had checked off the things already done.

I studied the list of things he had planned to do that day, noticed he had written the word "secret" three times, and wondered if it might have something to do with his now dead dumb dogie.

What'll I do with the list? I asked myself and kept on wondering what "secret" meant.

I also said to myself, *Bill Collins, if you hand the folded paper back to Little Jim, he'll know you read it. How else could you know it was his?*

"What'll I do?" I asked my Very Special Friend, the One who made boys. And even though there wasn't any voice answering, it seemed He wanted me to hand the list back to Little Jim and not show it to Poetry or to anybody else.

I left my little hay room and climbed down the ladder to the barn floor to hurry up and gather all the eggs. Then I would go into the house. I was going to sneak upstairs to see if Mom had made my bed yet. If she hadn't, I might decide to surprise her.

I hadn't any sooner reached the barn floor than my eyes caught a flash of black-and-white cat leaping from Dad's tool cupboard toward something on the floor by the window. And almost as quick as greased lightning, old Mixy had a mouse in her mouth.

5

As soon as I had finished gathering the eggs, I took them to the house and, when Mom wasn't looking, tiptoed upstairs. Instead of feeling disgusted with Little Jim for being such a good boy, I was proud of him for giving me a good idea.

Because I had the maybe the best mother in the whole world, I ought to try to prove to her that she had one of the best sons. I could hardly wait till Mom would find out what I was going to do and thank me for it.

About as quick as you can say, "Scat," to a cat, I was through. I gave my pillow three or four fast final socks with my fist to smooth it out a little better and was just tucking in the spread at the foot of the bed when I heard Mom come into the house from outdoors somewhere. Straining my ears in the downstairs direction, I heard her moving toward the stairway. In another minute, she might be on her way up to start doing what I had already done.

That was one of Mom's housekeeping rules —never to go anywhere away from home until the beds were made, the furniture dusted, and the dishes washed—not if she could help it.

"How come?" Dad had asked her many a

time, especially when he was in a hurry to get started and she wasn't ready yet.

And Mom always had the same answer: "You never know who might come home with us or stop in to see us, and I don't want any woman to think I am a careless housekeeper."

The bed finished and the spread straight enough for any woman to see it, I quick started toward the north upstairs room so that, when Mom would get to the top of the stairs, she wouldn't see me. Instead, she would see the bed so well made that not a boy in the world would think I was a careless housekeeper.

I hadn't thought about there being anything on the floor needing to be picked up, though. And when I stumbled over my baseball glove and went down in a noisy *thumpety-bumpety-plop*, Mom's voice flew up the stairway, asking, "That you up there, Bill! What on earth!"

"Not what on earth," I called down to her, "but what on the floor!" Trying to be funny and not being, I added in my raised voice, "Somebody's son left his baseball glove right where I would stumble over it! What a dumb bunny!"

"While you're up there," Mom ordered me, "would you like to make up the bed? You never know who might drop in to see us, and I don't want any woman thinking I'm a careless housekeeper."

Now, I ask you, what can a boy do when he has just done something thoughtful for his mother and she, not knowing he has just done it, orders him to do it?

For some reason, I was angry inside and for the next half hour or more had a hard time being as good a boy as I thought I was.

As soon as supper was over and all the chores were finished, we were almost ready to go to town. That is, Dad was ready, and I was ready. So also was Charlotte Ann, in Dad's arms in the car. Mom was still in the house doing last-minute woman's stuff, so that if anybody came home with us—and you know the rest of what I was thinking right that minute.

"What you locking the door for?" Dad called when she at last came out but was stopping to lock the back door, which hardly anybody in Sugar Creek territory ever does.

"Cattle thieves!" Mom called. She tucked the key in her handbag and came on out to the car.

In a few minutes we were on our way to town.

It was, as you already know, Saturday night, when, as Mom often expressed it, "everybody and his dog would be there." Everybody and his dog weren't there, of course, but there certainly were a lot of people. Some of the mothers had come to get the Saturday night bargains in the grocery stores and to see what woman had a new hat or was going to buy one. The fathers had come to drive the family cars and see their friends. The young people were there because other young people would be there. And the Gang came because we liked each other and the Saturday night excitement.

We met as we had planned, in front of the Pop Shop, not far from the town's drinking fountain. We were nearly always thirsty, not for the lukewarm water that spurted up out of the fountain on a hot night, but for ice-cold soda pop in bottles.

Inside the Pop Shop we could also get our shoes shined, buy candy bars, and just stand around and talk.

I got one of the most interesting surprises a boy ever got in his life, when, watching my chance, I took Little Jim around the corner of the Pop Shop and handed him the folded piece of paper I'd found on the floor of the cave.

He looked at me as if he had been shot at and missed, as he quickly took the paper and shoved it into his shirt pocket. It was the same pocket, I noticed, that had had the handkerchief he'd lent to Big Jim in the afternoon. *That,* I thought, *explains how the note happened to get out of his pocket in the first place.*

He stood for a minute, not saying anything, and as much as I wanted to know what the word "secret" meant, which he'd written three times on his list of things to do that day, I waited to see if he would tell me.

"Well," he asked, "don't you want to know what my secret is?"

"What secret?" I replied innocently.

"I put an ad in the paper," he told me. "I offered a reward for anybody who found Wandering Winnie to bring her home and get a ten-dollar reward."

With that, Little Jim took out his billfold and handed me a clipping from the daily paper that nearly all the Sugar Creek families take. And there it was—except that there it wasn't.

I could hardly believe my eyes when I read:

LOST. A white-faced heifer. If found, return her to the James Foote farm for a $100.00 reward.

"That," I told him, "is not ten dollars! That's a hundred dollars! Look!"

He looked and was as surprised as I was. "What'll I do if they do find her and bring her back? Where'll I get a *hundred dollars!*"

"Yeah—where?" I said. Then I added, "But they won't. You know and I know where Wandering Winnie is right this very minute. In a gunnysack in the Sugar Creek swamp."

"Maybe she's not," he said hopefully. "Maybe that's some other white-faced calf. I've been praying that—"

He stopped, gulped, and—well, that's how I found out the real secret. Anybody who knows Little Jim knows he is maybe the best Christian boy in the whole Sugar Creek territory and that he had made the same kind of promise to God that I had—to read from the Bible and pray every day of his life.

Do you know what? That wonderful little guy's secret was this: he was praying a special prayer for Wandering Winnie to be found and brought back. This is the way he wound up explaining it to me: "I promised that if I do get her back, I'll trade her for a Korean orphan."

Well, my mind flew back to the sermon we'd had in our church the week before. Our pastor had told us that anybody could "adopt" his own orphan for only fifty dollars a year.

Also, I remembered Dad's prayer that very morning when he had said, "And help us to do what we can about the hungry orphans over there."

Imagine! That wonderful, cute, littlest member of our gang was willing to trade his orphaned calf for an orphaned human being! The little dogie he liked almost as much as he would a little brother—he not having any brother to love or play with.

"But it's no use to pray for her now. Not if she's already dead," he said with a smothered sob in his voice.

He swallowed as if there was a lump in his throat, then gave his head a quick toss to get the tears out of his eyes. That was the way he nearly always did it, so that nobody would see his tears and think he was a girl or just a little kid who cried easily.

Back inside the Pop Shop we went, where I bought Little Jim a bottle of his favorite soda and stood studying the two mottos on the south wall of the shop. They said:

> DON'T SWEAR!
> I HONOR THE NAME
> YOU TAKE IN VAIN.

and

IF YOU EXPECT TO RATE
AS A GENTLEMAN,
DO NOT EXPECTORATE
ON THE FLOOR.

Poetry, who had his flash camera with him, hanging by a strap around his neck, took two or three pictures of the wall mottos as different members of the gang stood under them. He took one of me with a bottle of pop going down my throat, while I looked toward the ceiling,

Then he and I went outside and moseyed around a little, walking in and out and round and round the square the way most of the rest of the people were doing. While we walked, we talked and kept our eyes and ears open to see if we could see anybody that looked like a calf-napper.

By the time we came back to the Pop Shop, the rest of the gang had left and were maybe walking round and round and in and out as we had been doing. And then is when Poetry grabbed me by the arm and pulled me back around the Pop Shop corner, hissing, "There she is! That's her!"

I quick looked where the jerk of his head told me to and saw a square-shaped woman in brown pants swinging along toward us. She was holding a cigarette with one hand and eating a candy bar with the other. When the plodding, square-shaped woman reached the corner where we'd been just before we'd darted around it, she made a sharp turn the other way.

Then she started on a catty-cornered stride toward the park and the gravel walk we knew went through the park to a part of town where there were a few empty store buildings and an abandoned blacksmith shop. There, before there had been automobiles, all the farmers from all over everywhere took their horses to get them fitted with new horseshoes. People didn't take their horses there anymore but their worn-out or wrecked automobiles. There were maybe thirty-five cars and trucks in a large lot by the old blacksmith shop.

There was a lamppost at the entrance of the park. After that, the path was dark all the way through. The town council had voted to put lights along the winding path but had not done it yet on account of what is called "politics," my father had told my mother one night last week, and I had overheard it.

Anyway, several seconds and maybe seven steps before the woman disappeared into the park, walking slowly and whistling some kind of tune, she finished all the cigarette she wanted to and flicked the stub toward the lamppost, where it fell and rolled a few feet to a smoking stop in the gravel walk.

Poetry and I must have had the same idea. As soon as she was gone, we hurried as fast as we could, without seeming to be hurrying, over to the light. There I stooped as though I was going to tie one of my shoes. Actually I did untie and tie it again, and while I was that close to the ground, I saw a green-tipped cigarette stub with red lipstick on the end of the filter.

Wow!

When you are for sure on the trail of a calf-napper who has stolen and butchered your best friend's prize baby beef, stuffed its red hide and white head in a burlap bag, and tossed it into the quicksand of the Sugar Creek swamp—I say, when you are absolutely sure you are on the trail of the calf-napper, what do you do?

Poetry decided for us, saying, "Let's take the shortcut to the bridge and hide behind the spirea there and take her picture!"

Before I could have said no even if I had wanted to, I took off after him in a fast run across the dark park and past a sign that said Keep Off the Grass, which we were going to keep off of as soon as we could.

Two fast boys can outrun a strolling woman any day, so we were crouching behind the spirea bush maybe two minutes before we heard her feet coming toward us on the gravel walk.

It was a tense minute. We didn't even dare whisper, or one or the other might say, *"Shh!"* That shush might be louder than the whisper, and we might miss getting the woman's picture.

Right then Poetry did shush me, though, for the pinkish white flowers of the spirea bush made me sneeze.

Now we could really hear her heavy steps. In another very few seconds she would be at the bridge, the bulb of Poetry's flash camera would explode in her face, and we'd have the picture we wanted.

Crunch . . . crunch . . . crunch . . .

Nearer and nearer and still nearer those steps came.

And then—just when she was close enough for Poetry to quickly stand up, spring out onto the walk, and take the picture—there was a stealthy movement behind the spirea on the *other* side of the walk, not more than fifteen feet from us, as though somebody else was waiting there.

In that spine-tingling second, Poetry pressed his camera button.

In that split second of on-and-off-again blinding light, I saw a big, husky man as block-shaped as the woman. He had a long, bushy, reddish brown beard and was bareheaded. Poetry had taken a picture of a woman *and* a man.

"Quick! Under the bridge!" Poetry ordered.

We ducked down the steep embankment. But then we had to stop, because the place where the Gang sometimes used to sit in the shade on a hot summer day and talk and tell stories, eat candy bars, and make plans and stuff—the place was full of hissing, fast-flowing water from the afternoon's rainstorm!

Well, Poetry's flashbulb must have stirred up the man's temper. His beard-bordered mouth was spouting some of the filthiest words a boy ever heard. Also, he had a flashlight and was shining it all around in fast circles, trying to spot us.

It seemed like the right time to do what Poetry just then ordered us to do, which was, "Run for your life!"

And we did—each one running for his own life—not back toward the lights of Main Street, which was a lot farther, but across the bridge toward the other side of the park, where it seemed it would be easy to lose ourselves among the old abandoned cars and trucks.

It was ridiculous at such a scary time to be thinking about a story we had in our school reader. But while we were running for our lives and the flashlight of the red-bearded man was trying to focus on us, making it hard for us to keep out of his sight, and while his curses were still in my ears, I was thinking about Peter Rabbit running for his life with the hot-tempered Mr. McGregor chasing him.

I was also remembering the wall motto in the Pop Shop that said DO NOT SWEAR! I HONOR THE NAME YOU TAKE IN VAIN.

And it seemed that maybe the wickedest thing a person could do was to use the Creator's Name the way the red-bearded man was doing it.

We darted into the abandoned car lot and worked our way along a row of oldish Fords, Buicks, Chevies, and other makes. As soon as we thought it was safe, we stopped, panting and listening.

"They've got to be here somewhere," I

heard the woman's husky voice say and then heard the man's guttural answer, "Let 'em go! Maybe they didn't take a picture. Maybe that was just a flashlight."

A second later, they passed us and began looking farther along.

"Now," Poetry whispered in my ear, "let's hide in the blacksmith shop. We can climb in through the back window."

It was a good idea, except that we hadn't figured on the front fender of somebody's old car to be lying in the way and two boys stumbling over it.

Clankety-rattlety-clatter!

Down we went and up we got, with Mr. and Mrs. McGregor after us again!

"I saw them run toward the blacksmith shop!" I heard the woman say, and we knew that even if we could get there and inside, we would be like two rats in a trap.

Spotting a pickup truck in the alley leading to the blacksmith shop, we scooted across a shadowy place, ducked around to the back of it, and, because we had to have a place to hide, quick climbed up into the truck bed. We crouched low, panting and holding our breath. And even in the middle of what could be real danger, I was still thinking of Mr. McGregor and Peter Rabbit—Peter jumping up and in and hiding inside a tall sprinkler can.

As quiet as two scared-half-to-death mice with a hungry cat after them, we waited and listened. We hoped the red-bearded man and the woman would go away so that we could spring out and make a beeline back across the park to Main Street—to where the rest of the gang were and where the picture Poetry had taken could be left with the Pop Shop owner for developing.

Right then I began to have a hard time with my olfactory nerves. I was crouched on what seemed to be a pile of empty gunnysacks. They smelled as if they had had bran shorts in them, and I had to fight off a noisy sneeze by pressing my fingers against my upper lip under my nose.

Then a light turned on in my mind as I realized for sure what I was smelling—a gunnysack like the kind that right that very second had a calf's hide and head in it and was lying at the edge of the quagmire in the Sugar Creek swamp!

"You smell what I smell?" I whispered to Poetry, but he shushed me.

I kept on fighting a want-to sneeze.

The tense seconds dragged past as if they were minutes, while we waited and listened and smelled and wondered why things were so quiet all of a sudden.

A moment later, we found out. A car went past on the park's back street, and a spotlight from the car cut through the darkness, its long shaft searching all around.

Poetry hissed in my ear, "The sheriff's after them!"

It might have been a good time for us to leap out of the pickup and start running and yelling and crying, "Help! Help!"

But before I had time to think such a fast, worried thought, the sheriff's car went on. To yell now would be to let the red-bearded man and the stocky woman, who was maybe his wife, know where we were. Two boys would be caught in a pickup instead of in a blacksmith's shop, and we'd probably get the living daylights knocked out of us.

Then is when we heard footsteps running in our direction and heard the two doors of our truck open and close.

A split second later the motor started, the truck leaped forward, and we shot out of that alley like thunder on wheels. The truck swung into Park Road, skidded around a corner, and headed for the moonlit country.

What on earth in a pickup truck—and why? And also, *where to?*

6

What a ride!
      One thing was for sure: our pickup
wasn't any old worn-out truck somebody had
left in the wrecker's junkyard. They had only
parked it there because it was a good hiding
place. The pickup had a powerful motor, and it
was being driven at one of the fastest speeds I'd
ever ridden in my life.

It wouldn't be safe for us to jump out. A boy
could get killed jumping out of a fast-moving
car. The only thing we could do that was safe
was to lie quiet and wait for the truck to stop.
Then maybe we could get out, and if we were
in any part of the territory we knew, we could
find our way back to town or to one of our
houses and phone the sheriff or the police.

I was still smelling bran shorts and gunnysacks and thinking about Wandering Winnie.
Poetry and I kept on lying with our heads close
to each other's so we could say anything we
thought it was safe to say.

"Know where we are?" Poetry said into one
of my ears.

And I answered, "We're on pavement yet. I
think we're on the road that goes past the
church—and the cemetery," I added, thinking
one of the saddest thoughts a boy ever thinks.

Faster and faster, it seemed, we flew along that paved highway.

"We're going downhill now," Poetry said, and almost at the same time there was a *rattle-bangety-bang* clattering noise as the wheels of the car went flying across a wooden-floored bridge.

Now I knew for sure where we were. The only wooden-floored bridge left in the county was the one that crossed Wolf Creek at the foot of the hill below the church.

On and on and still on. And hurry and worry and wonder and wait and hope. That was all that was going on in my mind.

Yet not quite all. I should have guessed we weren't the only passengers in the back of that pickup. Ever since we had plopped ourselves in, I had been having a hard time with my olfactory nerves. I had been smelling not only bran shorts, which cows and calves like to eat so well, but *something else*.

I found out what when I reached over to touch Poetry on the shoulder so that I could get his attention and tell him something. My hand missed his shoulder and slipped through a crack in a crate that was standing between us and the truck's cab. And what with my wandering hand did I feel but the warm hair and hide of something alive!

At the same time, I heard a sound that was not the roaring motor or the flying tires of the pickup we were in. It was the half-smothered bawl of a calf. I say "smothered," because it was the kind of a bawl a cow or calf makes when it doesn't open its mouth but lets the sound come out through its nose.

Now I knew for sure we were on the trail of a calf-napper. I told Poetry what I had just thought.

And he said back, "Not just calf-nappers, but boy-nappers! We're being stolen, too, you know!"

Already our truck was up the hill on the other side of the board-floored bridge and moving fast toward the area that was the playground of the Sugar Creek Gang. It was near to where we all lived and not far from the lane that leads to the creek, the sycamore tree, the cave, and the swamp.

Then Poetry muttered in my ear a plan his mind had just come up with. "When they stop to butcher this one, we'll jump out before they do and hide. While they're actually skinning it, we'll snap another picture, then run like lightning for whoever's house we're nearest to and phone the sheriff."

It was a good plan—or would have been if our captors had driven past our house and on toward the lane that leads toward the swamp. But they didn't.

Instead, when they came to the lane that angled off toward Little Jim's house, they swung into it, and the pickup picked up speed as they sped us on a *jouncety-shakety-bumpety-bump-bump* ride along the edge of our south pasture.

At a time like that you can't think straight, but because you *have* to keep still, you do it, though every drop of blood in your body is tingling with wondering what will happen next.

On my right, across our south pasture, I could see my house, where I knew there was a phone, and which I was planning to run to and use as soon as I had a chance.

Any minute, I thought, we'd come to wherever they had butchered Little Jim's Wandering Winnie. There the truck would slow down, swing off into the woods, and the butchering of another calf would begin.

But I thought wrong. We kept going right on until we came to the wide-spreading maple tree that shaded the gate at Little Jim's house! There our captors turned in and stopped right beside Little Jim's yard gate, not far from their summer kitchen and the side porch of their house.

If Poetry and I were going to get out of the pickup without being seen, now was the time.

Talk about fast movements. Two boys—a red-haired slender one and a blondish round one—were up and out of that pickup's wagon box in less time than it takes me to write it and were scooting for a hiding place behind the lilacs at the side of the house.

Peering through the lilac leaves, I saw the woman open the truck door on her side and, with a flashlight in her hand, hurry toward the Footes' porch. Then I heard her knock at the door.

At the same time Poetry was whispering in my ear a plan of some kind, which, because my mind was divided, I could hardly hear. Part of what I did hear was, "You wait here with the camera until I get back and yell, 'Now!' Then snap the picture."

With that, he handed the camera to me and took off along the row of lilac shrubs that bordered the house, leaving me wondering what on earth. What he was going to do, I didn't have the least idea, on account of not hearing his plan. But I did know how to use his flash camera, so I waited in a cringing crouch to see what would happen and to snap the picture whenever he ordered me to.

When nobody answered the woman's knock, which nobody could because nobody was home, the woman knocked again.

I said, "Nobody could," but I was wrong. Right that very second the door did open a crack and somebody did answer, and believe it or not, it was good old Poetry, asking, "Yes? Who's there?"

I guess maybe every member of the Sugar Creek Gang knew like an open book the inside of the house of every other member. That's why Poetry could race around Little Jim's house, slip in the back door, and find his way through to the front door so fast.

That, I thought, was the plan he had whispered in my ear a few fast minutes ago.

"We're looking for James Foote," the woman with the flashlight said, though I could hardly hear her for the noise of the pickup's motor still running in the drive. "We saw your ad in the paper and decided the calf that had strayed onto our place was yours. We have it here in the truck."

What a disappointment! All this time, I had thought we were riding in a cattle rustler's pickup and that the man and woman were wicked people. Now, it seemed they were innocent ranchers, who lived somewhere in the territory. Wandering Winnie had wandered over to their place, and they were bringing her home again.

Poetry's answer was as surprising as what the woman had just said. "I'm the only one here right now. But the folks ought to be home pretty soon. If you'll just put the calf in the corral . . ."

"We came to claim the reward," the woman said. "We'll wait."

Poetry's voice had a doubt in it when he answered, "Are you sure you've got the right calf? Was it a white-faced Hereford?"

The woman's answer was very polite as she said, "Of course! Come, take a look!"

While I waited, wondering what on earth was in Poetry's mind—and how come everything had changed—that heavyset woman led Poetry to the pickup and shined her light on the crate in the truck bed. From as far away as I was, still looking through the lilac leaves, I saw a live, red-haired calf with an all-white face. I also saw that there was a muzzle on the calf so it wouldn't be able to open its mouth and let out any long, high-pitched, trembling bawl as I'd heard Little Jim's dumb dogie do so many times in the neighborhood.

Poetry, still pretending to be a member of the Foote family, took quite a while to climb up into the truck and out again. While he was there, using the woman's flashlight, he examined Wandering Winnie's face and neck and ears, like a mother looking over her son's Saturday night bath.

When my detective-minded friend shuffled out of the truck, he said, "I'm satisfied. Maybe I can get the folks to come home right away. Wait a minute while I use the phone." With that, Poetry started back to the house. But on the way, he circled the lilac and whispered to me his secret.

"It's like I thought. That's not Wandering Winnie. Winnie had a scar over her left eye where she got cut on the barbed-wire fence at your place. Remember?"

I remembered.

He whispered something else before going into the house to make the phone call. "I think they're the thieves and they've stolen another calf just to get the reward. I'm going to phone the sheriff."

It was a tense minute, I tell you, while I waited in the shadows and fought to keep from sneezing on account of the very fragrant flowers of the lilacs. The truck's motor was still running and its lights still on, lighting up the

Footes' empty corral, where Wandering Winnie used to be kept. The woman was also using her flashlight, zigzagging it here and there across the lawn and then swinging it back to the house door again just in time to catch Poetry's face as he came out.

"You're to take the calf over to the Collinses. They'll keep it there tonight in their corral. I'll ride along and show you where."

With that, Poetry started down the steps, stumbled over his feet, and rolled over a couple of times till he was behind the lilac bush where I was. "The phone's out of order," he whispered to me. "We'll have to stall for time. The minute we're out of the drive, you beat it for your house and phone the sheriff to come there!"

Then he rolled onto his feet again and came up limping, saying, "I've got to fix that old step tomorrow morning."

That thought was good thinking, because the bottom step of the porch did need fixing.

I knew for sure how keen a mind Poetry had, when, instead of the truck's going back down the lane the way we had come—which would be the shortest way around to our house —they drove north toward the Sugar Creek School. To go that way would be almost two miles and at least five minutes farther.

If I ran like a cottontail with seventeen hounds after it, I could get to our house and in and have the sheriff's office on the phone before Poetry and the rustlers with the calf could come driving up to "Theodore Collins" on our mailbox.

After that, we could stall them a little longer while they waited for James Foote to come with the reward money—which he wasn't coming with—and we'd capture ourselves a couple of cattle rustlers.

Run . . . Run . . . Run . . . Pant . . . Pant . . . Pant . . . Hurry . . . Hurry . . . Hurry . . .

Across Little Jim's lawn I flew, through their lawn gate, down the lane to the stile over which I went *lickety-sizzle,* through our melon patch, then past the twin pignut trees, and on to our barnyard. I had to get to the phone quick—real quick! Would I get there quick enough?

7

That was a good question. Would I be able to get home to our phone quick enough to get the sheriff called before Poetry, the rustlers, and the stolen calf would come driving up to "Theodore Collins" on our mailbox?

And after I called the sheriff, would he be able to drive from town fast enough to get to our house quick enough to arrest the rustlers before they got tired of waiting for James Foote, who wasn't coming anyway?

Worrying wouldn't help, I knew. But running would.

And so I ran—as I already told you—down the lane from Little Jim's place all the way to the stile the gang used almost every day in fall, winter, and spring, going to and from school. Then I went up and over the stile.

With all that worry on my mind, it was ridiculous to remember the lady in our school-book who had so much trouble with a pig that wouldn't go over a stile. But with every flying step, the words went racing along in my mind: *"So he went a little further till he met a rat, and he said, 'Rat, rat, gnaw rope, rope won't hang butcher, butcher won't kill ox, ox won't drink water, water won't put out fire, fire won't burn stick, stick won't beat dog, dog won't bite pig, piggy won't go over the stile, and I shan't get home tonight. But the rat wouldn't, so he went a little farther till he saw a cat . . .'"*

And right then, I myself saw a cat. She was at the garden gate, waiting to catch a mouse maybe, and she went scooting ahead of me to the iron pitcher pump and on to the kitchen door—and I did get home that night.

I opened the screen, turned the doorknob to go in, and then remembered. Mom, who had been worried about people who steal calves right out of your backyard on your front doorstep, had locked the door, and the key was in town in her handbag!

Like a streak I was around the house to the front door, hoping it wouldn't be locked. But it also was!

And now what on earth! I *had* to get inside to use the phone to call the sheriff.

Well, I knew where we kept the extra key, so I looked in the secret place no one outside our family is supposed to know. And . . .

The key began to turn the lock, the boy began to turn the knob, the door began to open, and the boy began to race for the phone where he began to take it off the hook to see if the party line was busy—and it was!

I mean it really was. Three or four women were talking and worrying to each other about all the excitement there was in the neighborhood. One of them said, "I've been trying to call the Footes all afternoon, ever since the storm, but their phone seems to be out of order."

"Listen," I called into our own phone. "I've got to have the line! I want to call the sheriff! We're about to catch the cattle rustlers, and—"

But it wasn't any use. One of the women said to another woman, "Whatever is coming over people nowadays! Trying to get the line by scaring people!"

My temper fired up good and hot right then, and I yelled into the phone, "*Ladies, please!* This is Bill Collins! I've got to call the sheriff!"

Even though it is maybe the hardest thing in the world to get a woman to stop talking to or listening to another woman, all of a sudden it seemed those two or three or four women did believe me, and they did all hang up, and I *did* call the sheriff, and the lady in the office said she would send out a message to the patrol car, wherever it was.

I quick hung up then, hurried outdoors to the front gate, and opened it for the truck with the rustlers, the calf, and Poetry to drive in when they got there.

Then, with the flash camera ready to shoot, I hid behind the yellow rosebush.

Any minute now, the pickup might come hurrying up the road. Would the rustlers get here before the sheriff? My own folks were probably looking all over town for me. Poetry's folks would be doing the same thing for him. And hundreds of the rest of the people who were still in town would be still walking around and talking about things that didn't amount to very much, while Poetry and I with the help of the sheriff were capturing the rustlers who had been stealing livestock right out of people's backyards on their front doorsteps.

I saw the pickup's lights coming from the direction of the north road corner before I heard its engine.

Boy oh boy!

Now they were slowing down at "Theodore Collins" on our mailbox.

Now they were turning in, making a cloud of white dust, and stopping in our drive beside the plum tree.

Now also, things—what seemed maybe a hundred things—began to happen fast.

Say, have you ever watched a football game when the players are scattered all over the field? One man has the ball and is running with it, and almost before you can say, "Jack Robinson," half the men on both teams are all together in one place in a big pileup of legs and arms and helmets and grunts and groans, with the man with the ball somewhere under the whole pile!

That was the way things began to happen at the Theodore Collins place almost that very second. Down the road, shooting like a rocket with a flashing red light and a screeching siren came the sheriff's car. Behind it came another car and another and another. Two or three cars came whizzing up from the other direction— which is why you never know what will happen when three or four women who are on the phone at the same time tell their husbands what they've just heard.

There hadn't been so much grown-up excitement around our place in a long time.

From where I was in the moonlit dark, I could see Poetry in the pickup's bed, standing behind and holding onto the crate with the calf in it. And then, as the pickup lunged forward, he lost his balance, went down in a tangle of arms and legs, and rolled out onto the ground in front of the sheriff's car's headlights.

And at that very second, Poetry yelled above the noise of all the cars, "*Now!* Get the picture!"

And I got it! I rushed out to where he was, stopped, took aim and shot, wondering at the same time what he wanted a picture of himself for, lying on the ground in front of the sheriff's car, while the rustler's pickup went roaring across our barnyard toward Lady MacBeth's pasture bars.

Then the truck crashed into and through the bars and shot out into our south pasture, following the row of elderberry bushes that lined the fence.

Poetry rolled quickly out of the headlights of the sheriff's car, and that car leaped forward after the pickup, its siren going full blast through our barnyard, giving chase to the truck with Wandering Winnie's substitute in it.

For about seven minutes, more or less, there was a wild chase out there in our moonlit south pasture. The pickup was like a mouse in a house with a woman with a broom after it.

Then it headed back, its motor roaring, toward the pasture bars again. And that's when the accident happened.

Whoever was driving the pickup must have been pretty nervous or scared, because, instead of zipping through the gate, it whammed into the big corner post Dad and I had set up earlier that summer, and there it came to a fender-and-grille-smashing stop.

The sheriff's car, its spotlight lighting up the whole scene, screeched to its own stop right behind it. There were loud, sharp orders out there and threats, and the very nice man and woman who had only wanted to be kind to a boy who had lost his calf by bringing it home to him were captured.

It was nearly eleven o'clock before things quieted down at our house. The rustlers had been taken off to the county jail until it could be decided what to do with them. The neighbors who had heard me phone the sheriff and had come driving over to see what was going on—and to get in on the excitement—had gone home. And the Collins family was ready to settle down for a long summer's nap.

In my room, before tumbling into bed, I looked down at the moonlit crazy-quilt bedspread and said, "What a waste of work! Even though you never know who might come home with you or stop in to see you, if nobody got to see the very neat way a boy could make his bed, it was a very sad shame!"

My prayer was maybe even shorter than the one I usually prayed at night, and only a few of the words of it stayed with me after I sailed off with Wynken, Blynken, and Nod into a sea of dew.

Early the next morning when I went out to our south pasture to drive in Lady MacBeth for Dad to milk her, I couldn't find our contented Holstein anywhere!

Two or three times I let out a long, high-pitched cow call. What, I asked myself, had happened to *her*? Had all last night's excitement been too much for her nervous cow temperament and she had run away?

"But she couldn't get out!" I mumbled to myself, remembering the strong, new pasture bars I had just crawled through—the ones Dad had put there last night after the old ones had been smashed into giant-sized matchsticks when the pickup crashed through them.

"Sw-o-o-o-o-o-ok! Sw-o-o-o-oook!"

Still there wasn't any black-and-white cow in sight—not until I looked under the elderberry bushes along the fencerow. And what to my still half-sleepy eyes should appear but Lady MacBeth, lying on her side and chewing her cud. Lying beside her, also chewing her cud, was a white-faced Hereford that was the same size as and looked exactly like Wandering Winnie!

"What on earth!" I said out loud. "Where in the world did *you* come from?"

But when I took a closer look, there wasn't any barbed-wire-made scar above the long-eyelashed left eye.

Well, before noon that day, Little Jim had a brand-new Hereford calf to take the place of Wandering Winnie, who would never come home again. The neighbors, as soon as they found out what was in the gunnysack in the swamp, had chipped in and bought a substitute calf for him.

The gang didn't get to do what we'd planned to do the day before—which was draw straws to see who got to climb out on the over-hanging branch above the quicksand. We did get to watch one of the sheriff's men do it, and we did get to satisfy ourselves that Wandering Winnie had really been rustled and butchered. The white calf's head in the old burlap bag had a scar over its left eye.

After the sheriff and his men had driven away to town, the gang had a get-together in the shade of the beech tree near the Black Widow Stump.

Lying on our sides like contented cows chewing on grass stems, we listened to each other explain all the exciting things that had happened the exciting day and night before.

We were so busy and noisy talking that we hardly noticed the humming and buzzing of ten thousand bees gathering honey from the creamy yellow flowers of the leaning linden tree or the cheerful robins ordering us to cheerily, cheerily go jump in the lake.

Little Jim, grinning proudly, said to all of us, "It's a good thing I put that ad in the paper."

Dragonfly's answer was a little sarcastic, but it was the truth, anyway, as he answered, "It's also a good thing you didn't know how to write ten dollars but offered a hundred-dollar reward instead. The rustlers would never have stolen another heifer to try to make you think it was your own dumb dogie."

"I did know the difference," Little Jim defended himself. "It was just a mistake"—which it seemed I ought to believe it was.

After our meeting broke up, and Little Jim and I were alone, he said to me, "I won't feel so bad selling Winnie the Second this fall and adopting an orphan with the money, now that I know for sure my own Winnie is dead and I'll never see her again, anyway."

With that, Little Jim picked up a flat stone he found lying on the ground and gave it a long hard toss in the direction of Sugar Creek, like George Washington trying to throw a silver dollar across the Potomac River.

I watched that flat stone sail high out over the leaning linden tree until it reached the top of its curve and dropped down with a splash into Sugar Creek's foam-freckled face, starting a circle of waves that spread out and out in every direction there was.

It certainly felt good to be a boy and to be alive on such a wonderful sunshiny day.

The day seemed even more wonderful right

after supper when I went out to feed Old Red Addie and her fine family of six red-haired pigs.

I tossed maybe seventeen ears of corn over the fence for their supper, and as I watched them come running and squealing to eat them, I focused my eyes on the reddest-haired one of all, the one Dad had given me when the litter had been born.

"You," I said to that very fat little porker as he started eating like a pig one of the biggest ears of corn there was, "are going to market next fall so a little orphan boy in Korea can have roast beef once in a while."

Feeling something brushing against my bare ankle, I looked down. It was old Mixy, stroking her soft black-and-white fur against me the way cats like to do.

All of a sudden I got one of the gladdest feelings ever a boy can get. I quickly stooped, scooped Mixy up in my arms, and, pressing my cheek against her soft fur, said, "You're the nicest cat in the world—absolutely the nicest!"

But my scooping her up so fast scared the daylights out of her. She came to the fastest cat life I'd ever seen her come to in any of her nine lives. First, she shot out of my arms like a four-legged black-and-white arrow, straight for the hole that goes under the south side of our barn. And there she shot herself in—the way she always does when a neighborhood dog is chasing her.

The *Sugar Creek Gang* Series: